Published by Ladybird Books Ltd
A Penguin Company
Penguin Books Ltd, 80 Strand, London WC2R 0RL, England
Penguin Books Australia Ltd, 250 Camberwell Road, Camberwell, Victoria 3124, Australia
Penguin Group (NZ), cnr Rosedale and Airborne Roads, Albany, Auckland, New Zealand

Meg and Mog Television Series copyright © Absolutely/Happy Life/Varga 2003
Based upon the books featuring the characters Meg and Mog
by Helen Nicoll and Jan Pieńkowski
Licensed by Target Entertainment
This book based on the TV episode **Meg's Fancy Dress**
Script by Carl Gorham
Animation artwork by Roger Mainwood
First published by Ladybird Books 2005
6 8 10 9 7
Copyright © Absolutely/Happy Life/Varga, 2005
All rights reserved
LADYBIRD and the device of a ladybird are trademarks of Ladybird Books Ltd
Printed in Italy

# MEG & MOG

## Meg's Fancy Dress

Ladybird

MEG & MOG
created by
Helen Nicoll and Jan Pieńkowski

The witches' fancy dress party was going to take place that night on Witches Hill. Meg got out the dressing-up box to look for a costume.

"I need something very pretty and very grand," she told Mog and Owl.

She tried on her outfit. "What do you think?"

"Did you say something pretty?" chuckled Owl.

"Something grand?" giggled Mog.

"Well, I haven't got anything else," said Meg.

"Maybe a spell would help,"
suggested Mog.

So Meg stirred her cauldron.

"Rum dee dum,
 Craft by hand,
 Make me an outfit
 That's pretty and grand."

There was a flash of lightning and a cloud of smoke. Suddenly they were out in the countryside and Meg had been transformed into a lovely princess. Mog and Owl were impressed.

"Now that is pretty," said Owl.

"And grand," said Mog.

"Just what I wanted," said Meg.
"Fancy dress party here I come."

From near at hand there was
a roaring noise.

"What was that?" asked Mog.

"It's a dragon," said Owl.

"Don't dragons eat princesses?"
asked Mog.

This one certainly seemed keen to
get his teeth into Meg.

"RUN!" everyone shouted.

The dragon was gaining on them.

"Do another spell, Meg, quick!"
pleaded Mog.

Meg kept running but she tried
another spell.

"Fido dum
And fiddledy dee,
Give me a costume
To set us all free."

There was another flash and a big puff of smoke and the dragon disappeared. But so did Meg's princess costume. Instead she had turned into a prehistoric cavewoman.

"That's a funny costume," said Mog.

"I preferred being a princess," said Meg. "But at least no dragon will want to chase me now."

"No," said Owl, as an even louder roaring noise started, "but I think that woolly mammoth will."

And sure enough a woolly mammoth was galloping over the hill and heading straight for Meg.

"RUN!" they all shouted.

The woolly mammoth soor
to catch them up.

"Another spell, Meg!" c

"Fido dum
And fiddledy dee,
Another costume
To . . . whooah!"

Just in time a cloud of smoke
covered them. When it cleared away
Meg was looking very different.

Mog shouted with laughter. "You're a banana!"

"Well," said Meg, "it's not pretty and it's not grand, but absolutely no one's going to chase me now."

"Don't speak too soon," said Owl, as a fierce-looking gorilla came barging through the trees with his eyes on Meg's delicious banana costume.

"RUN!" they all shouted.

"Another spell, Meg!" yelled Mog.

**"Fido dum
And fiddledy . . . whooah!"**

With a flash and a bang they were
on the top of Witches Hill.

But something very odd had
happened to Meg's costume.
She was wearing the princess's
headdress, the banana's body and
the prehistoric cavewoman's shoes.

Then Meg noticed something else.

The dragon, the woolly mammoth and the gorilla were circling the top of the hill, all looking hungrily at Meg's outfit.

"Oh no!" said Meg.

The dragon let out a terrible roar.
Then his head tilted back and a
friendly face peered out at them
from inside.

"Hello, Meg," said Bess the witch.
"I was trying to catch you up but
you kept running away."

The woolly mammoth raised itself
and out of its front half came Jess
and from its back half came Tess.
The gorilla took off its head and
there was Cress.

"It's only us, Meg," said the witches.
"It is supposed to be a fancy dress
party, after all!" And everyone
laughed.

Then the dragon, the woolly mammoth, the gorilla and the prehistoric banana princess danced till dawn on Witches Hill and had the best fancy dress party ever.